Snow White

Jacob (1785–1863) and Wilhelm (1786–1859) Grimm are commonly known the world over as the Brothers Grimm (*die Brüder Grimm*). They were German academics and authors who specialised in collecting and publishing folklore during the 19th century. They popularised stories such as Rapunzel, Snow White (*Sneewittchen*), Hansel and Gretel (*Hänsel und Grethel*), and Rumpelstiltskin (*Rumpelstilzchen*). Their first collection of folk tales, "Children's and Household Tales" (*Kinder- und Hausmärchen*), was published in 1812.

The rise of romanticism during the 19th century revived interest in traditional folk stories, which represented a pure form of national literature and culture to the brothers. With the goal of researching a scholarly treatise on folk tales, they established a methodology for collecting and recording folk stories that became the basis for folklore studies. Between 1812 and 1857, their collection was revised and republished many times, growing from 86 stories to more than 200.

The popularity of the Grimms' collected folk tales has endured well, and the tales are available in more than 100 languages and have been adapted by many filmmakers.

SNOW WHITE
The Original Brothers Grimm Fairytale

JACOB & WILHELM GRIMM

Brothers Grimm's
'Children's and Household Tales'
No. 53

FIRST EDITION
Translated by Rachel Louise Lawrence

Blackdown
PUBLICATIONS

This translation of the Brothers Grimm "*Sneewittchen*" from '*Kinder- und Hausmärchen*' (First Edition, 1812) first published in 2014 by Blackdown Publications; this revised and extended edition, including "*Sneewittchen*" from '*Kinder- und Hausmärchen*' (Seventh Edition, 1857), first published in 2020

ISBN-13: 978-1074705541

Illustrations on front cover by Carl Offterdinger (1829-1889)
Interior illustrations by Franz Jüttner (1865-1926)

Aarne-Thompson-Uther [ATU] Classification of Folk Tales
II. 300-749: Tales of Magic
    II.vii. 700-749: Other Tales of the Supernatural
        II.vii.viii. 709: Snow White

CONTENTS

Snow White

THE ORIGINAL BROTHERS GRIMM FAIRYTALE

SNOW WHITE

First Edition

Brothers Grimm's
'Children's and Household Tales'
No. 53

Chapter One

The Wishes of a Queen

O nce upon a time in the middle of winter,
when the snowflakes were falling like
feathers from the sky, there sat a
beautiful Queen sewing in a window, which had
a frame of black ebony. As she worked, gazing
out on the snow, she pricked her finger with the
needle and three drops of blood fell upon the
snow.

Seeing how beautiful the red looked on the
white snow, the Queen thought to herself, *If only*

I had a child as white as snow, as red as blood, and as black as this frame.

Time passed and soon after the Queen had a little daughter, whose skin was as white as snow, cheeks as red as blood, and hair as black as ebony, and therefore she was called Little Snow White.

The Queen was the most beautiful woman in all the land and very proud of her beauty. She had a magic mirror, which she would stand in front of every morning and ask:

"Mirror, mirror on the wall,
Who in this land is fairest of all?"

And the magic mirror always said:

"You, my Queen, are the fairest of all."

And then the Queen knew for certain that there was no one more beautiful than she in the land.

However, Little Snow White grew up and when she was seven years old, she was so beautiful that she surpassed even the beauty of her mother, and when the Queen asked her magic mirror:

"Mirror, mirror on the wall,
Who in this land is fairest of all?"

The magic mirror replied:

"You, my Queen, are the fairest here, it is true;
But Little Snow White is still a thousand times
    fairer than you!"

As the Queen heard the mirror speak such words, she turned pale with envy, and from that moment on, she hated Little Snow White, and whenever she looked at her, she thought to herself, *Snow White is to blame that I am no longer the most beautiful woman in all the land*, and her heart turned against her daughter.

The envy within the Queen gave her no rest, and so she summoned a huntsman and said to him, "Take Snow White out into the woods, to a remote spot far from here, and stab her to death. As proof you have carried out the deed, bring back to me her lungs and liver, which I will cook with salt and then eat."

Chapter Two
The Kindness of Strangers

The huntsman took Little Snow White and led her to a secluded spot in the woods. When he had drawn his hunting knife and was about to stab her, Little Snow White began to cry. "Let me live, dear huntsman," she begged, "and I shall run deeper into the woods and never return."

The huntsman took pity on her because she was so beautiful and thought to himself, *The wild beasts will soon devour her. I do not need to kill her, and for that I am glad.*

As Little Snow White fled, a young wild boar came running by and the huntsman stabbed it to death. He cut out its lungs and liver before returning to the palace and handing them over to the Queen as proof of Little Snow White's demise. She cooked them with salt and ate them, all the while thinking she ate Little Snow White's lungs and liver.

Meanwhile, Little Snow White wandered through the great forest, all alone. She soon became quite afraid and began to run. She ran over sharp stones and through grasping thorns all day long.

At last, as the sun was about to set, she came to a small cottage. The cottage belonged to seven dwarfs who were not at home but at work in the mines.

Little Snow White went inside, where she found everything small but clean and tidy. Upon a little table, there were seven little plates, with seven little spoons, seven little knives and little forks, seven little cups, and against

7

the wall stood seven little beds, each one freshly made.

Little Snow White, hungry and thirsty, ate a few vegetables and a small amount of bread from each little plate, and drank a drop of wine out of each little cup. Then, because she was so tired, she wanted to lie down and go to sleep. So she tried each of the seven little beds, one after another, but none suited her until she came to the seventh one, which was just right. So she lay down in it and fell asleep.

When it was night, the seven dwarfs came home from working in the mine, and, when they lit their seven little candles, they saw that someone had been in their home.

The first dwarf said, "Who has been sitting in my little chair?"

The second said, "Who has been eating from my little plate?"

The third said, "Who has been eating my bread?"

The fourth said, "Who has been eating my vegetables?"

The fifth said, "Who has been stabbing with

my little fork?"

The sixth said, "Who has been cutting with my little knife?"

The seventh said, "Who has been drinking from my little cup?"

Then, after looking around, the first dwarf said, "Who has stepped on my bed?"

Then the second said, "Someone has been lying in my bed."

And so said all until the seventh dwarf, who looked at his little bed, and upon finding Little Snow White lying asleep within it, he said, "Someone is lying in my bed!"

At his cry, the other dwarfs came running, and they cried out in astonishment. They fetched their seven little candles and looked at Little Snow White.

"Oh, goodness! Oh, goodness!" they cried. "What a beautiful girl!"

The dwarfs were so delighted by Little Snow White that they did not wake her, but left her on the little bed to sleep peacefully. Meanwhile, the seventh dwarf slept with his companions, an hour with each one, until the night was over.

When Little Snow White awoke, one dwarf asked her, "Who are you?"

Another asked, "How did you come to be in our cottage?"

"My name is Snow White," she said, "and I am here because my mother tried to have me killed, but her chosen huntsman spared my life, and so I ran all day until finally, I came to your little cottage."

The dwarfs took pity on her and one said, "If you will keep house for us—by cooking and sewing, washing and knitting, making our beds and keeping everything clean and tidy—then you can stay with us and you will want for nothing."

"We come home in the evening," said another, "and our supper must be ready to eat upon our return. But during the day, we are digging for gold in the mine, and you will be alone."

"You must be on the lookout for the Queen," warned another, "and do not let anyone enter the cottage."

Chapter Three
The Trickery of a Queen

The next morning, the Queen stepped before the magic mirror and, thinking that she was once again the most beautiful woman in the land, asked:

"Mirror, mirror on the wall,
Who in this land is fairest of all?"

The magic mirror replied:

"You, my Queen, are the fairest here, it is true;
But beyond the seven mountains dwells

Little Snow White, who is alive and well,
And she is a thousand times fairer than you!"

When the Queen heard this, she was startled, and she knew at once that she had been deceived, that the huntsman had not killed Little Snow White. Since no one but the seven dwarfs lived in the seven mountains, the Queen knew at once that Little Snow White must have been saved because of them.

Now, she plotted anew how she would kill Little Snow White, for so long as the mirror would not say that she was the most beautiful woman in the land, she would have no peace.

Though the Queen was uncertain about a great many things, she decided what she would do next, and she disguised herself as an old pedlar woman. Colouring her face so that no one would recognise her, she went over the seven mountains to the cottage of the seven dwarfs.

She knocked on the door and cried out, "Open up! Open up! I am the old pedlar woman with good wares to sell!"

Little Snow White looked out of the window and asked, "What have you got to sell?"

"Staylaces, dear child," said the old woman, and she held up a lace that was woven from yellow, red, and blue silk. "Would you like to have it?"

"Oh, yes," said Little Snow White, and thought to herself, *I can let this good old woman inside, for she seems honest.* So, in good faith, she unbolted the door and bargained for the beautifully-woven laces.

"My, how sloppily laced up you are!" said the old woman. "Come, I will lace you up properly."

Little Snow White stood patiently before the old woman as she took the staylace and tied it so tightly that Little Snow White lost her breath and fell to the ground, as if dead.

After that, the Queen was satisfied and she went away.

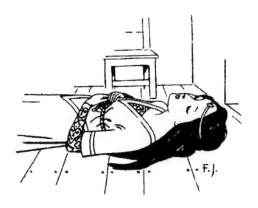

It was nightfall soon afterwards, and when the seven dwarfs came home, they were horrified to find their dear Little Snow White lying on the ground, as if she was dead.

Together, they lifted her, and when they saw

that she was laced up so tightly, they cut the staylace in two. Right away, she took a breath, and then she came to life again.

"There was no one but the Queen who wished to take your life," one dwarf said.

"Be careful," another added, "and do not let anyone enter the cottage again."

M eanwhile, the Queen asked her magic mirror:

"Mirror, mirror on the wall,
Who in this land is fairest of all?"

The magic mirror replied as before:

"You, my Queen, are the fairest here, it is true;
But beyond the seven mountains dwells
Little Snow White, who is alive and well,
And she is a thousand times fairer than you!"

The Queen was so shocked that all the blood in her body rushed to her heart when she understood that Little Snow White must have come to life again.

Then, all that day and night, she thought of how to bring about her daughter's demise until eventually, she decided to make a poisoned comb. She then disguised herself in the form of a completely different character, and she went over the seven mountains to the cottage of the seven dwarfs once again.

The Queen knocked on the door and Little Snow White called out, "I must not let anyone enter!"

The Queen then drew out the comb, and when Little Snow White saw how it gleamed, and that the seller was a stranger, she opened the door and bought the comb from her.

"Come, I will comb you as well," said the old woman.

But scarcely had she stuck the comb in Little Snow White's hair than the girl fell to the ground and was dead.

"Now, you will lie there forever," said the Queen, and as she went home, her heart grew lighter.

That night, the dwarfs came home just in time. They saw what had happened and pulled the poisoned comb out of Little Snow White's hair. She then opened her eyes and came to life again.

"I most certainly will not let anyone inside the cottage again," she promised the dwarfs.

In the meantime, the Queen stepped in front of her magic mirror and asked:

> "Mirror, mirror on the wall,
> Who in this land is fairest of all?"

The magic mirror again answered:

"You, my Queen, are the fairest here, it is true;
But beyond the seven mountains dwells
Little Snow White, who is alive and well,
And she is a thousand times fairer than you!"

When the Queen heard these words again, she began to tremble and shake with anger and she vowed, "You shall die, Snow White, even if it costs me my life!"

She then went into her most secret room, where no one was allowed to enter, and there she made a deadly poisonous apple. It was outwardly beautiful, white with red cheeks, and anyone who saw it would crave it.

The Queen then disguised herself as a peasant woman, walked to the cottage of the seven dwarfs, and knocked on the door.

Little Snow White looked out and said, "I am not allowed to let anyone inside. The dwarfs have expressly forbidden me from doing so."

"Well, if you do not want to let me in, I cannot force you," said the peasant woman. "I will sell my apples soon enough, but I can give you one to sample, if you wish."

"No, I must not take anything, even a gift," said Little Snow White. "The dwarfs do not want me to."

"You may well be afraid," said the peasant woman, "but I will cut the apple in two and eat half of it, and you shall have the beautiful red half."

The apple, however, was so cunningly made that only the red half was poisoned.

When Little Snow White saw that the peasant woman was eating her half of the apple, her craving for it grew ever more powerful. Finally, she let the woman pass the other half through the window and accepted it.

Little Snow White bit into the apple, but she scarcely had she taken a bite than she fell to the ground, dead.

The Queen rejoiced, went home, and asked the magic mirror:

> "Mirror, mirror on the wall,
> Who in this land is fairest of all?"

The magic mirror replied:

"You, my Queen, are the fairest of all."

"Now I have peace," she said, "for I am the most beautiful woman in the land once again, and Snow White will remain dead this time."

Chapter Four
A Glass Coffin and a Prince

In the evening, the dwarfs came home from the mines and found their dear Little Snow White lying on the ground, and she was dead.

They unlaced her and looked to see if they could find anything poisonous in her hair. But nothing helped—they could not bring her back to life.

The dwarfs laid out Little Snow White on a bier, and all seven of them sat down beside it and wept and wept for three days. They then intended to bury her, but they saw that she still looked vital, with her beautiful red cheeks, and not at all like a dead person. So they made a glass coffin instead and laid her inside it, so that she could be seen easily.

The dwarfs then inscribed her name and ancestry upon its sides in gold letters, and one of them remained at home every day and kept watch over her.

So Little Snow White lay in the glass coffin for a long, long time and did not decay. She was still as white as snow and as red as blood, and if her eyes could have opened, they would have been as black as ebony, for she lay there as if she was asleep.

One day, a young Prince came to the cottage of

the dwarfs and wanted to spend the night in it. When he entered the room and saw Little Snow White lying in the glass coffin, on whom seven little candles cast their light, he could not get enough of her beauty.

He read the golden inscription and saw that she was the daughter of a King. He then asked the dwarfs to sell him the coffin with the dead Little Snow White inside.

But the seven dwarfs would not part with it, not for all the gold in the world.

The Prince then asked them to give her to him, saying, "For I cannot live without being able to see her. I will hold her in high regard and honour her as the one most dear to me in all the world."

The dwarfs took pity on him and gave him the coffin, and the Prince had it carried to his castle and placed inside his room, where he sat by himself all day and could not take his eyes off her. And whenever he had to go out and could not see Little Snow White, he became sad and could not eat a morsel unless the coffin stood beside him.

However, the servants who had to carry the coffin around constantly became angry about doing so. One time, one of them opened the coffin, lifted Little Snow White upright, and said, "For the sake of a dead girl, we are tormented all day," and he thumped her on the back with his hand.

The poisonous piece of apple she had bitten off was then dislodged from her throat, and Little Snow White was alive once again.

Little Snow White then went to see the Prince, who did not know what to do with himself, he was so elated when he saw his dear Little Snow White alive. They then sat down together at the table and ate with delight.

Their wedding was arranged for the next day, and Little Snow White's wicked mother was also invited to attend.

When the Queen stepped in front of the magic mirror that morning and asked:

"Mirror, mirror on the wall,
Who in this land is fairest of all?"

The magic mirror answered:

"You, my Queen, are the fairest here, it is true;
But the young Queen is still a thousand times
fairer than you!"

When the Queen heard these words, she was shocked, and become so afraid that she could not say a thing. But her envy grew so much, it drove her to go to the wedding to see the young Queen. And when she arrived, she saw that the young Queen was indeed Little Snow White.

Next, iron slippers were heated in the fire, and the Queen was forced to put them on and dance in them. Her feet were miserably burned, but she was not allowed to stop until she had danced herself to death.

SNOW WHITE

Final Edition

Brothers Grimm's
'Children's and Household Tales'
No. 53

Chapter One

The Envy of a Queen

O nce upon a time in the middle of winter, when the snowflakes were falling like feathers from the sky, a Queen sat sewing at a window, which had a frame of ebony wood. As she sewed, she looked up at the snow and pricked her finger with the needle, and three drops of blood fell into the snow.

Seeing how beautiful the red looked in the white snow, she thought to herself, *If only I had a child as white as snow, as red as blood, and as black as the wood of this window frame.*

Soon after, she had a little daughter, whose skin was as white as snow, cheeks as red as blood, and hair as black as ebony, and was therefore called Little Snow White. And when the child was born, the Queen died.

After a year had passed, the King took another wife. She was a beautiful woman, but she was proud and conceited, and she could not bear it if she should be surpassed in beauty by anyone. She had a magic mirror, and when she stepped in front of it and looked at herself in it, she asked:

"Mirror, mirror on the wall,
Who in this land is fairest of all?"

To this, the magic mirror answered:

"You, my Queen, are the fairest of all."

Then she was satisfied, for she knew that the mirror always told the truth.

But Little Snow White grew up and became more and more beautiful, and when she was seven years old, she was as beautiful as the clear day and more beautiful than the Queen herself.

Once, when the Queen asked her magic mirror:

"Mirror, mirror on the wall,
Who in this land is fairest of all?"

It answered:

"You, my Queen, are the fairest here, it is true;
But Little Snow White is a thousand times
  fairer than you!"

The Queen was shocked and turned yellow and green with envy. From that moment on, whenever she saw Little Snow White, her heart heaved in her chest, she hated the girl so much.

Envy and pride grew higher and higher, like weeds in her heart, so that she had no peace, day or night.

The Queen then summoned a huntsman and said, "Take the child out into the forest, for I no longer want to have her in my sight. You shall kill her, and bring her lungs and liver back to me as proof that she is dead."

The huntsman obeyed and led Little Snow White out into the forest. When he had drawn his hunting knife and was about to pierce Little Snow White's innocent heart, she began to weep and said, "Ah, dear huntsman, let me live. I will run into the wild forest and never return home again."

Because she was so beautiful, the huntsman took pity on her and said, "Run away, you poor child." *The wild beasts will soon devour you*, he thought, and yet it seemed to him as if a stone had rolled from his heart because he no longer needed to kill her.

Just then a young boar came scurrying by and he stabbed it, cut out its lungs and liver, and then took them to the Queen as proof of Little Snow White's death. The cook had to cook them with salt, and the wicked woman ate them up, thinking that she had eaten Little Snow White's lungs and liver.

Chapter Two
The Hospitality of the Dwarfs

P oor Little Snow White was now all alone in the great forest, and was so frightened that she simply stared at all the leaves on the trees and did not know how to help herself.

She then began to run and run, over sharp stones and through unbending thorns, and wild beasts bounded past her, but they did her no harm. She ran for as long as her feet could carry her until it was almost evening, then she saw a little cottage and went inside to rest.

Everything was small inside the little house, but so neat and clean that it cannot be said otherwise. There was a little table with a white tablecloth and seven little plates, and each plate had a spoon, and there were seven little knives and forks, and seven little mugs. Against the wall were seven little beds, standing side by side and covered with snow-white sheets.

Because she was so hungry and thirsty, Little Snow White ate a few vegetables and bread from each little plate, and drank a drop of wine from each little mug, for she did not want to take everything from one alone.

Afterwards, because she was so tired, she lay down on a little bed, but none of them suited her—one was too long, another was too short—until at last the seventh one felt just right. And so she remained lying in it, commended herself to God, and fell asleep.

When it was quite dark, the masters of the little cottage came home. They were the seven dwarfs who delved into the mountains, mining for ore. They lit their seven little candles, and when it was light in the little cottage, they saw that someone had been inside it, for everything was not in the same order in which they had left it.

The first dwarf said, "Who has sat on my little chair?"

The second said, "Who has eaten from my little plate?"

The third said, "Who has eaten some of my bread?"

The fourth said, "Who has eaten some of my vegetables?"

The fifth said, "Who has stabbed with my little

fork?"

The sixth said, "Who has cut with my little knife?"

The seventh said, "Who has drunk from my little mug?"

Then the first dwarf looked around and saw that there was a small indent on his bed, and he said, "Who has stepped on my bed?"

The others came running and each one shouted, "Someone has been lying in my bed too!"

But when the seventh dwarf looked at his bed, he saw Little Snow White lying there asleep. He then called the others, who came running, and they all cried out with astonishment. They fetched their seven little candles and shone the light on Little Snow White.

"Oh, goodness! Oh, goodness!" they cried. "What a beautiful child!"

The dwarfs were so glad that they did not wake her, but let her continue to sleep in the little bed. And the seventh dwarf slept with his companions, an hour with each one, until the night was over.

When it was morning, Little Snow White awoke, and when she saw the seven dwarfs, she was scared. But they were friendly and one asked her, "What is your name?"

"My name is Snow White," she answered.

"How did you come to be inside our cottage?" another asked.

Little Snow White then told them all, saying, "My stepmother tried to have me killed, but the huntsman she chose spared my life. I ran all day yesterday until I finally found your little cottage."

The dwarfs came to a decision, with one saying, "If you will keep house for us—by cooking, making the beds, washing, sewing, and knitting."

"And if you will keep everything neat and clean," another continued, "then you may stay with us, and you shall want for nothing."

"With all my heart, I accept," said Little Snow White, and she stayed with them, keeping the house in order for them. In the mornings, they went into the mountains seeking ore and gold, and in the evenings, they returned home again, and their supper had to be ready for them to eat.

During the day, Little Snow White was alone, and the good dwarfs warned her, "Beware of your stepmother, for she will soon know that you are here. Do not let anyone inside the cottage."

Chapter Three
The Disguises of a Queen

T he Queen, meanwhile, having believed that she had eaten Little Snow White's lungs and liver, thought that she was again the first and most beautiful woman of all, and she stood before her magic mirror and asked:

"Mirror, mirror on the wall,
Who in this land is fairest of all?"

Then the magic mirror answered:

"You, my Queen, are the fairest here, it is true;
But Little Snow White is still alive and well,
Beyond the hills where the seven dwarfs dwell,
And she is a thousand times fairer than you!"

These words shocked the Queen, for she knew that the magic mirror spoke only truth, and so she knew that the huntsman had deceived her and that Little Snow White was still alive.

And so she thought, and thought again, how she would destroy her stepdaughter, for as long as she was not the fairest in all the land, envy would not let her rest.

And when at last she had made up her mind about what she would do, she coloured her face and dressed herself as an old pedlar woman, so that no one would recognise her.

In this disguise, the Queen went over the seven mountains to the home of the seven dwarfs, knocked on their door and cried out, "Beautiful wares for sale, for sale!"

Little Snow White peered out of the window and called out, "Good day, dear woman, what do you have to sell?"

"Good wares, beautiful wares," she answered. "Staylaces of all colours." And she took out one that was woven from colourful silk.

I can let this honest woman in, thought Little Snow White, unbolting the door and buying the pretty staylace.

"Child," said the old woman, "how you look! Come, I will lace you up properly."

Little Snow White was without guile and so stood before the old woman and let herself be laced up with the new lace. But the old woman laced her up so quickly and so tightly that Little

Snow White could not breathe, and she fell to the ground, as if dead.

"Now you are no longer the most beautiful," the Queen said and hurried away.

Not long afterwards, in the evening, the seven dwarfs came home, but how horrified they were when they saw their dear Little Snow White lying on the ground, and that she did not move, as if she was dead.

They lifted her, and seeing that she was laced too tightly, they cut the staylace in two. Then Little Snow White began to breathe a little and gradually came back to life.

When the dwarfs heard what had happened, one dwarf said, "The old pedlar woman was none other than the wicked Queen."

"Beware," said another, "and do not let anyone enter the cottage unless we are with you."

When the wicked Queen returned home, she went and stood before her magic mirror and asked:

"Mirror, mirror on the wall,
Who in this land is fairest of all?"

Then the magic mirror answered as before:

"You, my Queen, are the fairest here, it is true;
But Little Snow White is still alive and well,

Beyond the hills where the seven dwarfs dwell,
And she is a thousand times fairer than you!"

When she heard this, all her blood rushed to her heart and she was afraid, for she knew that Little Snow White had come back to life again.

"But now," she said, "I will devise something that will destroy you." And with the aid of witchcraft, which she understood, the Queen made a poisoned comb. She then disguised herself and took the form of a different old woman, and went over the seven mountains to the home of the seven dwarfs, knocked on their door and cried out, "Good wares for sale, for sale!"

Little Snow White looked out and said, "Go away, for I must not let anyone inside."

"Surely, you are allowed to look at it," said the old woman, pulling out the poisoned comb and holding it aloft. It pleased the girl so much that she let herself be deceived, and she opened the door.

When they had agreed on a price, the old woman said, "Now, I will comb your hair properly."

Poor Little Snow White did not think anything amiss and so she let the old woman do as she pleased. But no sooner had she put the comb into Little Snow White's hair than the poison took effect, and the girl fell to the ground, unconscious.

"You model of beauty," said the wicked woman, "now you are finished." And she went away.

Fortunately, however, it was soon evening, the time when the seven dwarfs came home. When they saw Little Snow White lying on the ground, they immediately suspected her stepmother, and so they searched her and found the poisoned comb.

Scarcely had they pulled out the comb than Little Snow White came to herself again, and told the dwarfs what had happened. They then warned her once more to be on her guard and not to open the door to anyone.

Back at home, the Queen stood in front of her magic mirror and asked:

> *"Mirror, mirror on the wall,*
> *Who in this land is fairest of all?"*

Then the magic mirror answered as before:

"You, my Queen, are the fairest here, it is true;
But Little Snow White is still alive and well,
Beyond the hills where the seven dwarfs dwell,
And she is a thousand times fairer than you!"

When the Queen heard the mirror's words,

she trembled and shook with anger. "Snow White shall die," she cried, "even if it costs me my life!"

She then went into a most secret, solitary chamber, where no one was allowed to enter, and there she made a deadly poisonous apple. Outwardly, the apple looked beautiful, white with red cheeks, so that anyone who saw it longed to have it. But anyone who ate a small piece of it would die.

When the apple was ready, she coloured her face and disguised herself as a peasant woman, and so she went over the seven mountains to the home of the seven dwarfs.

She knocked on the door, and Little Snow White stretched her head out of the window and said, "I must not let anyone inside. The seven dwarfs have forbidden me to do so."

"That is all right with me," answered the peasant woman. "I shall get rid of my apples soon enough. There, I will give you one."

"No," said Little Snow White, "I must not accept anything."

"Are you afraid of poison?" asked the old woman. "Look, I will cut the apple in two. You eat the red half, and I will eat the white one."

However, the apple was so cunningly made that only the red half was poisoned.

Little Snow White glanced longingly at the beautiful apple, and when she saw that the peasant woman was eating her part of it, she could resist no longer, and she stretched out her hand and took the poisonous half.

But as soon as she had a morsel of it in her mouth, she fell to the ground, dead.

The Queen then stared at Little Snow White with a gruesome look, and laughed aloud and said, "White as snow, red as blood, black as ebony wood! This time, the dwarfs cannot awaken you again."

And when she returned home and questioned her magic mirror:

"Mirror, mirror on the wall,
Who in this land is fairest of all?"

It finally answered:

"You, my Queen, are the fairest of all."

Then her envious heart was at rest, as much as an envious heart can be at rest.

Chapter Four
The Gift of the Dwarfs

When they came home in the evening, the dwarfs found Little Snow White lying on the ground, and she was no longer breathing. She was, in truth, dead.

They lifted her and examined her to see if they could find something poisonous. They untied her laces, combed her hair, and washed her with water and wine. But it all came to nothing—the dear girl was dead, and she remained dead.

They laid her on a bier, and all seven sat beside it and wept over her, and wept for three long days. Then they were going to bury her, but she still looked as fresh as a living person, and she still had her beautiful red cheeks.

"We cannot bury her in the black earth," one dwarf said, and they had crafted a transparent coffin made of glass, so that she could be seen from all sides. They laid her inside it, and wrote her name in golden letters upon it, and that she was a King's daughter.

They then placed the coffin outside, upon the mountain, and one of the dwarfs always stayed with it and guarded it. And the wildlife also came and mourned for Little Snow White; first an owl, then a raven, and finally a dove.

Now, Little Snow White lay for a long, long time in the coffin, and she did not decay, but looked as if she was asleep, for she was still as white as snow, as red as blood, and as black-haired as ebony wood.

It then came to pass that a King's son journeyed into the forest and entered the dwarfs' cottage, where he sought lodgings for the night. He saw the coffin on the mountain, and the beautiful Little Snow White inside it, and read what was written in golden letters upon it.

Then he said to the dwarfs, "Let me have the coffin, and I will give you whatever you want for it."

But the dwarfs answered, "We will not give it to you for all the gold in the world."

"Then give it to me as a gift," the Prince said, "for I cannot live without seeing Little Snow White. I will honour and revere her as my dearest one."

As he spoke, the good dwarfs felt sorry for

him and they gifted him the coffin.

The Prince now had it carried away by his servants on their shoulders. And it so happened that they stumbled over a shrub, and the shaking of the coffin dislodged from Little Snow White's throat the poisonous piece of apple which she had bitten off.

And it was not long before she opened her eyes, lifted the lid of her coffin, sat up, and was alive once more.

"My goodness! Where am I?" she cried.

The Prince said most joyfully, "You are with me," and he told her what had happened. He then said, "I love you more than anything in the world. Come with me to my father's castle and you shall become my wife."

Little Snow White was agreeable and accepted his proposal. She went with him, and their wedding was conducted with great pomp and splendour.

But Little Snow White's wicked stepmother was also invited to the celebration. After she had dressed herself in beautiful clothes, she stood in front of the mirror and asked:

"Mirror, mirror on the wall,
Who in this land is fairest of all?"

The magic mirror answered:

"You, my Queen, are the fairest here, it is true;
But the young Queen is a thousand times fairer
than you!"

The wicked woman uttered a curse and became so afraid, so frightened, that she did not know what to do with herself.

At first, she did not want to attend the wedding, but it did not give her any peace, and so she had to go and see the young Queen. When she entered, she recognised Little Snow White and, filled with fear and terror, she stood there and could not move.

A pair of iron shoes had already been placed onto the burning coals, and they were carried in with tongs and set in front of her. She was then forced to step into the red-hot shoes and dance until she fell to the ground, dead.

About the Translator

Rachel Louise Lawrence is a British author who translates and adapts folk and fairy tales from original texts and puts them back into print, particularly the lesser-known British & Celtic variants.

Since writing her first story at the age of six, Rachel has never lost her love of writing and reading. A keen wildlife photographer and gardener, she is currently working on several writing projects.

Why not follow her?

 /Rachel.Louise.Lawrence

 @RLLawrenceBP

 /RLLawrenceBP

/RachelLouiseLawrence

Or visit her website:
www.rachellouiselawrence.com

Other Titles Available

Madame de Villeneuve's
THE STORY OF THE BEAUTY AND THE BEAST
The Original Classic French Fairytale

Story by Gabrielle-Suzanne Barbot de Villeneuve

Think you know the story of 'Beauty and the Beast'? Think again! This book contains the original tale by Madame de Villeneuve, first published in 1740, and although the classic elements of Beauty giving up her freedom to live with the Beast, during which time she begins to see beyond his grotesque appearance, are present, there is a wealth of rich back story to how the Prince became cursed and revelations about Beauty's parentage, which fail to appear in subsequent versions.

ISBN-13: 978-1502992970

CENDRILLON AND THE GLASS SLIPPER
The French 'Cinderella' Fairytale

Story by Charles Perrault

Her godmother, who was a fairy, said,
"You would like to go to the ball, is that not so?"

When her father remarries, his daughter is mistreated and labelled a Cindermaid by her two new stepsisters. However, when the King's son announces a ball, Cendrillon finds her life forever changed by the appearance of her Fairy Godmother, who just might be able to make all her dreams come true...

ISBN-13: 979-8696046723

ASCHENPUTTEL, THE LITTLE ASH GIRL
The Original Brothers Grimm 'Cinderella' Fairytale

Story by Jacob and Wilhelm Grimm
First Edition

"Go to the little tree on your mother's grave. Shake it and wish for beautiful clothes, but come back before midnight."

In the Brothers Grimm's version of a persecuted heroine's struggle to escape the hardships she experiences following her widowed father's marriage to a cruel woman with two beautiful but mean daughters, there are impossible tasks and helpful birds, a new name and an ash-dress, a Prince and three balls, a wish-tree and dresses of silver and gold.

Can Aschenputtel find happiness and a future full of promise, or will her family succeed in keeping her as their cinder maid?

ISBN-13: 979-8590909308

HANSEL AND GRETEL
The Original Brothers Grimm Fairytale

Story by Jacob and Wilhelm Grimm
First Edition

*"Nibble, nibble, little louse!
Who is nibbling at my house?"*

Translated from the first edition, experience the tale of *Hansel and Gretel* in its original form, as brother and sister are abandoned in a great forest by their parents, only to discover that someone far more sinister than wild animals awaits them...

ISBN-13: 978-1657234604

Made in United States
Troutdale, OR
03/22/2025